The Village

The Footpath

Granny

The Cart Road

RED
RIDING HOOD

RED RIDING HOOD

Retold by
BEATRIX POTTER
Adapted from the French of Charles Perrault

Illustrated by
HELEN OXENBURY

FREDERICK WARNE

FREDERICK WARNE

UK | USA | Canada | Ireland | Australia
India | New Zealand | South Africa

Frederick Warne is part of the Penguin Random House group of companies
whose addresses can be found at global.penguinrandomhouse.com.

This book first published by Frederick Warne 2019

001

Printed and bound in Italy

A CIP catalogue record for this book is available from the British Library

ISBN: 978–0–241–37653–9

All correspondence to:
Frederick Warne, Penguin Random House Children's
80 Strand, London WC2R 0RL

Foreword from Helen Oxenbury

From the moment I first read the manuscript, I couldn't resist illustrating Beatrix Potter's retelling of Red Riding Hood. Her version of the story is so rooted in the English countryside – wildflower meadows, and copses of birch trees, and pea-sticks in village gardens, which are a joy to paint.

Potter's telling is quite different to the story I remember from my own childhood: it's much closer to Charles Perrault's original French story – with a darker ending ("and that was the end of little Red Riding Hood!" – what a blow!). But I think children like a little darkness in their stories. And although I don't like giving wolves a bad press I was, more than anything else, drawn to Potter's depiction of this sly, cunning fellow. I'm sure I have heard actors say how interesting it is to play a villain after a run of nice and normal characters, and I definitely felt the same about illustrating this wicked wolf. You can't get a much nastier character to draw and develop, and it was great fun to really get my teeth into it. He starts off scrawny and scheming and ends up hardly able to walk home, he's so full with Granny and Red Riding Hood in his tummy! So although the ending in Potter's manuscript is a little dark, I thought there was quite a lot of humour there too. And if you look carefully at my final illustration, I've chosen to offer an alternative ending for the squeamish and the faint of heart. No way would a wolf that fat be able to outrun the woodcutters . . .

ONCE UPON A TIME there was a village child who was so pretty – so pretty as never was seen.

Her mother was fair silly about her, and her granny was sillier still.

The good woman, her mother, made the child a little hood of scarlet flannel, and the scarlet set off her bonny black curls, like the flame-coloured leaves round the heart of a poppy flower.

Wherever she went she wore it; and folks called her *"Little Red Riding Hood"*.

ONE DAY her mother baked tea-cakes. "Come," said she, "come put on thy little red hood, and trot away to thy granny's. They tell me that she's poorly.

"Take her this scone, and a little pat of butter. Run along quick with the basket, and bring me back word how she does."

RED RIDING HOOD set off obediently with the basket. Her grandmother dwelt in another village.

The path led over hill and dale, through golden meadow sunshine, and under the flickering, leafy shadows of the birch trees.

THE MYRTLE smelled sweet in the warm, sunny glades, and the west wind blew softly through the wood.

It brought a cheerful sound – the clink of axes and voices of woodcutters singing at their work.

"Sing ash, sing oak, sing charcoal smoke!
Sing hey the merry gean cherry!
Lay beech and bark for the windward screen,
Blue smoke and hazel and copse-wood green,
Sing hey for the woodland merry!"

Another voice far off amongst the trees took up the song –

"Here's ash and oak for the broad axe stroke,
Hey down come the red gean cherry!"

The cheerful voices died away in the distance.

BUT NO ONE saw little Red Riding Hood.

By the wooden swing gate at the end of the wood,
hard upon the open meadow, sat a great grey wolf.

He rested his chin upon the bars of the gate,
and he listened to the woodcutters.

He was afraid of them. He durst not go home
to his bed in the thicket.

Neither durst he jump upon Red Riding Hood,
when she laid her hand on the swing gate.
He had eaten nothing for three days, and his
mouth watered when he looked at her.

But the woodcutters' jolly voices rang down the wind, and the slow, long crash of a falling tree.

"Child, where are you going?" said the gaunt grey wolf.

Now Red Riding Hood did not know that it is dangerous to talk to wolves.

"Sir," said she quite simply, *"I am going to my granny's. This is a tea-cake that my mother has made, and this is a little pat of butter."* She lifted the white cloth that was spread over her basket.

"Does she live far off?" asked the wolf.

"Oh yes indeed," said little Red Riding Hood. *"Right across this big meadow and beyond the mill. It is the last house in the village."*

"*Heigh ho!*" said the wolf, stretching himself.

"*I may as well go too and see her; I have nothing else to do.*

"I'll go by the cart road along the side of the wood. And you shall follow the footpath over the little bridge: let us try which road is shortest."

THE WOLF went up the cart road,
lippitty, lippitty, slouching along.

But as soon as he had turned the bend of
the fence, and was hidden by the trees –
he laid out his legs and he ran!

THE LITTLE girl
loitered near the gate;
she climbed on the
railing to gather nuts.

Then she wandered
along the footpath
over the meadow,
picking wild flowers
as she went.

She made a posy
for her grandmother.

And where the footpath climbed the brae, beyond the plank bridge, there were little scarlet wild strawberries among the grass – as red as holly berries, as red as the hood of little Red Riding Hood.

She gathered them in a dock leaf and put them in her basket.

AT LAST she reached the high-road
and at last she stepped out faster. But
the golden sunshine was very low, and
the shadows were long and slanting,
before she passed the mill.

Nobody
saw her
pass.

THE WOLF had run with all his might along
the shorter way.

When he came in sight of the mill, he jumped
over a ditch and hedge above the road and landed
on the hill-side.

He slunk along amongst the ferns and boulders.

He came down at the farther end of the village,
behind the old woman's cottage.

Through a broken wall and round the woodshed,
he slipped between the cabbages and pea-sticks.

His wicked eyes winked at the sun as he stood
in the porch under the honeysuckle.

He knocked at the door – Tap! Tap! Tap! –
very softly with the pad of his foot.

"*Who's there?*"

"*It's your little Red Riding Hood, Granny,*"
said the wolf in a mincing voice. "*I've brought
you a tea-cake and a little pat of butter.*"

The poor old grandmother, who lay ill in bed,
called out, "*Pull the bobbin and the latch will go up!*"

The wolf pulled; the door opened; he crept in.

And then he made a great spring over the
foot of the bed . . .

The wolf was very hungry; he'd had no food
for three days.

In a little less than no time there was nothing
left at all of Red Riding Hood's grandmother.

WHEN THE wolf had finished he still felt a little hungry.

He shut the door, put on the poor old woman's night cap and bed jacket, and he got into bed.

He hid under the blankets, pulling the quilt up to his eyes, and he waited for Red Riding Hood.

AFTER A WHILE someone tapped at the door. Rat-tap-tap!

"*Who is there?*" said the wolf from the bed.

Red Riding Hood was surprised to hear such a gruff, deep voice. But she thought that her grandmother must be hoarse with a cold, so she answered –

"It is I, Granny; little Red Riding Hood. My mother has sent you a tea-cake, and a little pat of butter."

The wolf made his voice as small as he could and said, *"Pull the bobbin; the latch will go up!"*

Red Riding Hood pulled and the door opened.

The wolf crouched down under the bedclothes.

Said he in his hoarse, deep voice – *"Put the tea-cake and the butter on the dresser. Take off your shoes, and sit beside me on the bed."*

Little Red Riding Hood took off her little muddy shoes. She scrambled up on to the bed to kiss her granny.

But she was very much surprised when the thing that she thought was her grandmother pushed back the quilt and blanket and sat up.

"What big, strong, hairy arms
you have got, Granny?"
said Red Riding Hood.

"The better to hug you,
my dear!"

"What big hairy ears
under your night cap?"

"The better to hear you,
little Granddaughter!"

"But, Granny – your eyes have turned yellow?"

"The better to see you, my pretty!"

"But, Granny, Granny – what big white teeth –"

And that was the end of little Red Riding Hood.

The Wolf

Red Riding
Hood

Woodcutters